Sidebar illustrations by Nika Lopert
English translation by Kristina Alice Waller
Design by Grafični atelje Visočnik

First published in the Slovenian language in 2018 by Založba Pivec, Maribor, Slovenia.
First published in the English language in 2020 by Holiday House Publishing, Inc., New York.
All Rights Reserved
HOLIDAY HOUSE is registered in the U.S. Patent and Trademark Office.
Printed and bound in March 2020 at Toppan Leefung, DongGuan City, China.
www.holidayhouse.com
First Edition
1 3 5 7 9 10 8 6 4 2

Library of Congress Cataloging-in-Publication Data

Names: Plohl, Igor, author. | Šonc, Urška Stropnik, illustrator. | Lopert, Nika, illustrator.
Waller, Kristina Alice, translator.
Title: Lucas at the Paralympics / Igor Plohl ; illustrated by Urška Stropnik Šonc ;
sidebar illustrations by Nika Lopert ; English
translation by Kristina Alice Waller.
Other titles: Rogi in Edi na paraolimpijskih igrah. English
Description: First edition. | New York : Holiday House, 2020. | "First published in the Slovenian language in 2018
by Založba Pivec, Maribor, Slovenia." | Audience: Ages 4–8. | Audience: Grades K–1. | Summary: "Lucas the Lion
discovers the Paralympics—where physically disabled world-class athletes exemplify strength, determination, and
courage"—Provided by publisher. Includes sidebars about how athletes who are blind, wear prosthetics, or use
wheelchairs compete in different events, as well as the history of the Paralympic Games.
Identifiers: LCCN 2019039885 | ISBN 9780823447657 (hardcover)
Subjects: CYAC: Paralympic Games—Fiction. | People with
disabilities—Fiction. | Athletes—Fiction. | Lions—Fiction.
Classification: LCC PZ7.1.P624 Luc 2020 | DDC [E]—dc23
LC record available at https://lccn.loc.gov/2019039885

ISBN: 978-0-8234-4765-7 (hardcover)

Lucas at the
PARALYMPICS

by Igor Plohl * illustrated by Urška Stropnik Šonc

HOLIDAY HOUSE • NEW YORK

This is Lucas. One day he fell from a ladder and injured his spine. Lucas hasn't been able to use his legs since then. He uses a wheelchair to move around.

Lucas loves sports.

Lucas has a special hand-powered cycle that he rides every day. He likes to go fast.

One day Lucas saw someone on a cycle just like his—and he was going even faster. Lucas tried with all his might to catch up.

"Hello!" said Lucas.

"Hello!" said the other cyclist.

If someone is paraplegic, it means that he or she cannot walk due to a spinal disease or injury and uses a wheelchair to get around.

The other cyclist was named Eddie. Eddie and Lucas decided to cycle together every day. Soon they were friends.

Eddie told Lucas about the Paralympic Games, games that are held every four years. The best athletes, all with disabilities, from all over the world, compete for bronze, silver, and gold medals.

The name Paralympic is made of two parts. *Para* comes from the Greek word meaning "parallel" or "alongside." And *[O]lympic* refers to the Ancient Greek town of Olympia, where the first Olympic Games were held. The Paralympic Games take place the same year and in the same place as the Olympic Games.

Two years later, Lucas and Eddie took a plane and flew halfway around the world to the Summer Paralympics. Thousands of athletes from more than a hundred countries arrived to compete in more than twenty sports.

The symbol of the Paralympic Games has three asymmetrical crescents colored red, blue, and green. The crescents symbolize movement, and the colors were chosen because they are the most common colors in national flags around the world.

There are both Summer and Winter Paralympic Games.

The Paralympics are for athletes who cannot compete at the Olympic Games, as it would not be a fair competition for them.

Thousands of spectators, both in the stands and in front of television sets at home, cheered for runners racing on the track. Some of the runners wore a prosthesis.

A prosthesis is a medical aid that is used to replace a missing body part. Paralympic runners use prostheses that are made specially for each athlete's unique running style.

Blind runners raced too. Some could see a little, and some couldn't see at all, so every runner wore a blindfold for fairness. Each blind athlete ran with a guide. A leather rope called a tether connected them.

 Sprint competitions are held for 100 meters, 200 meters, and 400 meters. In relay races, athletes compete in 4x100 meter and 4x400 meter events. The runners also compete in 800 meter races and in marathons. Disabled athletes also compete in such disciplines as the high jump, long jump, triple jump, discus throw, hammer throw, javelin, and shot put.

Blind athletes played goalball too.

Lucas had never seen a goalball competition before, and it was so exciting! The athletes were fully or partially blind and all wore blindfolds for fairness, as the blind runners did.

Three players on each side tried to throw a ball into their opponents' goal. Defenders used their whole bodies to protect their goal.

The ball had bells in it so players could hear where it was. The spectators had to be quiet so that the players could hear the bells.

 Blind people can also play soccer. A special feature of this sport is that all the players, except for the goalkeeper, are blindfolded. There are four blindfolded players and a goalie who has only a slight vision impairment or can fully see. It is the goalkeeper's responsibility to defend the goal and guide the players.

Eddie's friend Jake was in a para swimming race.
"Go, Jake!" Eddie shouted.
"You can do it!" Lucas called out.

In para swimming, the pool is the same size as at the Olympic Games. It is 50 meters long and 25 meters wide. There are special panels at the end of the pool that detect when a swimmer touches them. This gives an accurate measurement of swimming times.

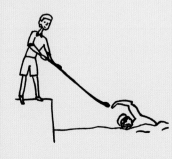

In para swimming, the athletes compete in freestyle, backstroke, breaststroke, butterfly, and medley events. Blind and visually impaired swimmers have assistants who use a special pole to warn the athletes when they are approaching the end of the pool.

Jake was very fast, but not fast enough to win a medal. He was very disappointed.

Lucas and Eddie tried to cheer Jake up. Jake thanked them for their support, but he didn't feel like talking. He knew he would feel better tomorrow, and in the days to come, he'd be happily training for his next competition. But for now, he just wanted to be alone.

Lucas and Eddie respected his wishes and watched him go back to the changing room.

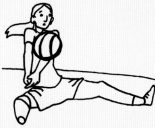

In sitting volleyball, the net is lower and the court smaller than at the Olympic Games. The competitors must always remain in a seated position when they come into contact with the ball, even if they are able to get up.

Wheelchair rugby is probably the roughest game at the Paralympics.

The next day, Lucas and Eddie watched athletes compete in sitting volleyball, wheelchair rugby, boccia, and para archery.

In boccia, a ball sport similar to bowling, the players are wheelchair users who have cerebral palsy, muscular dystrophy, or other neurological conditions. The players can throw the balls or roll them down a ramp.

Para archery has a long tradition. It was one of the sports in the first Paralympic Games in Rome in 1960.

Wheelchair basketball, where the hoop is the same height as in the Olympic Games, was very exciting. Players passed and shot the ball and went very fast. When they crashed to the ground, they picked themselves up without any help. Luckily the athletes were strapped into their wheelchairs.

The rules of wheelchair basketball are much like the rules in the Olympic Games. There are only a few differences: Players can give two pushes to their wheelchairs before they have to pass the ball. Intentionally crashing into another player is forbidden, as is traveling backward if it gets in the way of an opposing player. There is also a height restriction for wheelchairs: the height of the seat may not exceed 53 centimeters or 21 inches.

Wheelchair table tennis looked very difficult.
The athletes needed to control the wheelchair
with one hand and the paddle with the other.

In wheelchair table tennis, the ball
can bounce twice before a player
has to hit it. The court is the same
size as in the Olympic Games, and
the net is the same height.

Wheelchair fencers wore suits and masks that electronically detected when a sword touched them. Their wheelchairs were attached to the ground.

There are three different swords used in wheelchair fencing: foil, épée, and sabre. The fencer's wheelchair is attached to a frame that allows the athletes to move a little, and keeps the athletes the same distance apart.

The first Winter Paralympic Games were held in 1976 in Sweden. These were also the first Paralympics where athletes other than wheelchair athletes competed.

On the last day of the Paralympic Games, Lucas and Eddie went to a party with the athletes and their coaches. At the party, Lucas talked to an athlete who was going to be competing in para cross-country skiing at the next Winter Paralympics.

When Lucas returned home, he decided to practice for the Paralympic Games that would take place in four years. Even if he didn't qualify, he would have a lot of fun trying!

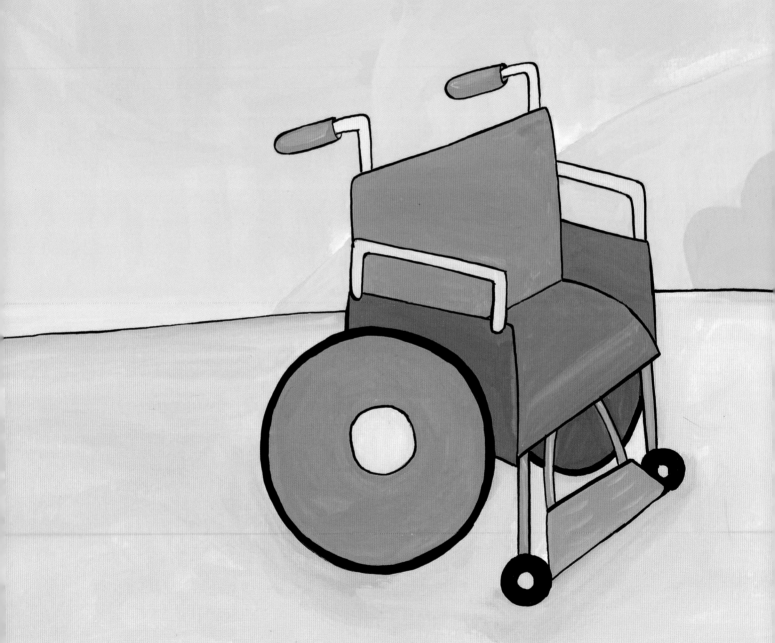

Paraplegic and other disabled athletes with motor impairments compete in cycling using hand-powered bicycles. Blind and visually impaired athletes can compete using tandem bicycles, where a guide who can see sits in front. Competitions also take place with regular bicycles and with tricycles for people who have problems with balance.

The Winter Paralympics

The winter sports include para alpine skiing, para cross-country skiing, para ice hockey, para snowboarding, and wheelchair curling.

 Para ice hockey is played in a sitting position on a special sled. Athletes move using their arms and two sticks that are also used to hit the puck.

 Athletes who use a prosthesis to walk can use regular skis. Athletes who are blind can ski with the help of a guide who skis in front and uses audio signals.

 Para alpine skiing evolved from the efforts of disabled veterans in Germany and Austria after World War II. Athletes with disabilities can compete in the following categories: slalom, giant slalom, super giant slalom, downhill, and combined.

 Para cross-country skiers compete in three events ranging from 2.5 kilometers to 20 kilometers long. The competition has two categories—classic and freestyle. Skiers who are blind or have a visual impairment compete using a guide.

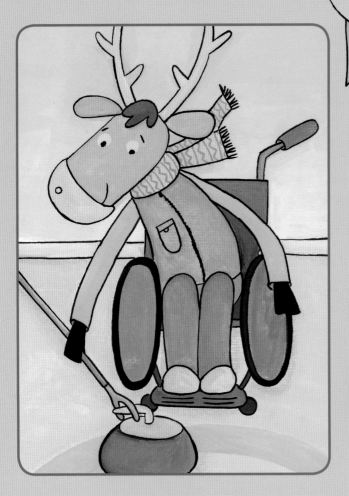

Wheelchair curling uses the same stones and the same playing surface that are used in the Olympic Games. Players use a special stick to push the curling stones and can also move the stones with their hands.

Athletes with motor impairments ski in the sitting position on a monoski. The seat is customized to each skier.

Para snowboarding is one of the newer Paralympic events. It made its debut at the Sochi Paralympic Games in 2014.

About the Author

Igor Plohl (pronounced EE-gor PLAHL) was born and raised in Slovenia, where he teaches at a primary school and lectures extensively on physical disability and spinal cord injury. After falling from a ladder at the age of twenty-nine, he injured his spinal cord and became paraplegic. He shares his experience in an autobiographical book for adults and in three children's books. You can learn more about Igor Plohl at igor-plohl.info.